The Dog and the Fox

by Jenny Jinks
illustrated by Hannah Wood

The Dog and the Fox

Maverick
Early Readers

'The Dog and the Fox'
An original concept by Jenny Jinks
© Jenny Jinks

Illustrated by Hannah Wood

Published by MAVERICK ARTS PUBLISHING LTD

Studio 3A, City Business Centre, 6 Brighton Road,

Horsham, West Sussex, RH13 5BB

© Maverick Arts Publishing Limited July 2017

+44 (0)1403 256941

A CIP catalogue record for this book is available at the British Library.

ISBN 978-1-84886-293-7

arts publishing
www.maverickbooks.co.uk

Yellow

This book is rated as: Yellow Band (Guided Reading)
This story is decodable at Letters and Sounds Phase 3.

The sun is up and so is Dog.

Dog is bored. He wants to play.

Dog gets a ball and runs to Fox.

"Get up," says Dog.

But Fox does not.

Dog digs up a bone.

It is big.

"Get up," says Dog.

But Fox does not.

Dog runs in the sun.

He gets hot.

"Get up," says Dog.

But Fox does not.

Dog jumps in the pond.

He is wet.

"Get up," says Dog. But Fox does not.

Dog sits in the sun.

He is worn out.

"Get up," says Dog.

But Fox does not.

The moon is up and so is Fox.

Fox is bored.

He wants to play.

Fox gets a ball and runs to Dog.

"Get up," says Fox.

But Dog does not.

Quiz

1. The sun is up and...?
a) So is Fox
b) So is Frog
c) So is Dog

2. What does Dog take to Fox?
a) A ball and a bone
b) A boot
c) A cake

3. Why does Dog get hot?
a) He jumps in a pond
b) He runs in the sun
c) He walks with Fox

4. Where does Dog jump?

a) In the mud

b) Into bed

c) In the pond

5. What is Dog doing when Fox wants to play?

a) Sleeping

b) Running

c) Digging

Turn over for answers

Book Bands for Guided Reading

The Institute of Education book banding system is a scale of colours that reflects the various levels of reading difficulty. The bands are assigned by taking into account the content, the language style, the layout and phonics.

Maverick Early Readers are a bright, attractive range of books covering the pink to purple bands. All of these books have been book banded for guided reading to the industry standard and edited by a leading educational consultant.

For more titles visit:
www.maverickbooks.co.uk/early-readers

 Pink

 Red

 Yellow

 Blue

 Green

 Orange

 Turquoise

 Purple

Book Band
Yellow

Little Fish and Big Fish	978-1-84886-292-0
Sheep on the Run	978-1-84886-291-3
The Dog and the Fox	978-1-84886-293-7
Can I Have My Ball Back?	978-1-84886-252-4
Izzy! Wizzy!	978-1-84886-253-1

Quiz Answers: 1c, 2a, 3b, 4c, 5a